DILLY
THE WORST DAY EVER

'Dilly,' she said, 'I think you must be the naughtiest, most stubborn little dinosaur in the whole, wide world . . . I don't think you could be good for a whole day if you tried.'

'I could, I could!' shouted Dilly.

'All right, Dilly,' said Mother. 'If you think you can, why don't you prove it? Why don't you try and be good for the rest of today? And if you are good, perhaps we'll give you a little treat . . .'

Tony Bradman

DILLY
THE WORST DAY EVER

Stories of the World's Naughtiest Dinosaur

Illustrated by Susan Hellard

MAMMOTH

First published in Great Britain 1988
by Piccadilly Press Ltd
Magnet paperback edition first published 1989
Reissued 1990 by Mammoth
an imprint of Mandarin Paperbacks
Michelin House, 81 Fulham Road, London SW3 6RB

Mandarin is an imprint of the Octopus Publishing Group

ISBN 0 7497 0540 X

A CIP catalogue record for this title
is available from the British Library

Printed in Great Britain
by Cox & Wyman Ltd, Reading, Berkshire

CONTENTS

I. DILLY AT THE LIBRARY

Did I ever tell you about the time Dilly
was naughty at the library? I'll never
forget it, and I don't think the dinosaurs
who work there will either.

I love going to the library, because I
love books. I can read really well, now –
at school I'm on Level 8 Readers. At
home I like reading the books about *The
Famous Five Dinosaurs*. They're great.

Dilly loves books too, but he can't
read yet, so Mother and Father still have

1

to read to him. He likes picture books and stories about big bad creatures who chase little dinosaurs and try to gobble them up.

Sometimes we go to a bookshop to *buy* books. And sometimes we go to the library to *borrow* books. The only problem is that Dilly doesn't understand the difference.

"Come on, Dilly," said Father one day. "Get your books together. We've got to take them back today so you can get some new ones."

"But I don't want any new ones, Father," said Dilly. "I want to keep the books we bought at the library last week. They're mine."

"No, no, Dilly," Father laughed. "You don't *buy* books at the library. You only *borrow* them. You have to take them back once you've read them, so other people can read them too."

I could see that Dilly was looking
rather confused.

"So do we have to take back the
books we get from the bookshop, too?"
he said.

"No, Dilly," said Father. "You *buy*
books at the bookshop, so you can keep
them forever. Do you understand now,
Dilly?"

"Yes, Father," said Dilly. "I
understand."

But I don't think he did. He still
looked very confused, and at the library,
he did what he usually does – he

borrowed the same books he'd had before. Father tried to get him to have some new ones, but Dilly didn't want to.

"Are you sure you want the same books, Dilly?" Father said.

"Yes, Father," said Dilly. "They're my books, and I'm taking them home with me."

A week or so later, it was time to take our library books back. Father didn't even try to explain to Dilly about the difference between borrowing and buying. He just got the library books together and told Dilly that we were going.

"What's that you've got there, Dilly?" said Father just as we were leaving. Dilly was clutching a book under his arm.

"It's *The Three Little Dinosaurs*, Father," he said. Father sighed.

"That's not a library book, Dilly," he

4

said. "We *bought* that book at the Shopping Cave yesterday."

"I know, Father," said Dilly. "I just want to take it with me."

It took Father a while, but in the end he managed to persuade Dilly to leave *The Three Little Dinosaurs* at home.

Dilly was very well behaved at the library. He told Father that he would quite like to have some new books, this time, some books that he'd never read before. So he sat at a small table in the children's library looking through lots of different books while I chose mine. Father asked me to keep an eye on Dilly while he went into the grown-ups' library to choose his books, and get some for Mother, too. I said I would.

After a while, Father came back and said that it was time to go. I had the books I wanted, and Dilly had chosen his. We went to the counter where the librarian stamped everyone's books.

The library was crowded that day, so there was quite a queue. We were waiting behind another family, a Mother, Father and one small dinosaur who looked about the same age as Dilly. She was holding a book against her chest. She smiled at me, and then at Dilly.

But Dilly didn't smile back. I could see that he had a very strange look on his face, too. He looked rather cross. The little dinosaur stopped smiling, and backed towards her parents.

"Where did you get that book?" said Dilly. "It's mine!"

"No it isn't," said the little dinosaur. "It's mine!"

"Give it to me," said Dilly. He reached towards her and tried to grab the book.

"You can't have it!" said the little dinosaur. "I won't let you!"

"Hey," said Father. "What's all this about? Don't be naughty, now, Dilly. It isn't your book. You've chosen yours, so leave the little dinosaur alone." He smiled at the little dinosaur's parents. Everyone in the queue was starting to look at us.

"But it is, Father," said Dilly. "It is my book!" Father looked quite cross now.

"I don't know how many times I've told you, Dilly," he said, "but you must try to understand. You can't keep the books you borrow from the library. Even if you've had that book before, it doesn't belong to you."

Dilly looked at Father . . . at the little dinosaur . . . and at everyone around him. I knew what was going to happen, and you do too, probably. He opened his mouth and . . . he let rip with an

ultra-special, 150-mile-per-hour super-
scream, the sort that makes librarians
duck under counters, grown-ups hide
behind the shelves, and little dinosaurs
bump into a big stack of books that fall
over. A grown-up tripped over the
books on the floor, and fell against some
more shelves . . . and they were
knocked over, too. By the time Dilly
had finished screaming, the library was
in an awful mess.

Father was very cross, and gave Dilly quite a telling off. I saw the little dinosaur looking at Dilly, and then I noticed what book she was holding.

It was *The Three Little Dinosaurs*.

Dilly thought she had his favourite book, the one he'd left at home! I told Father, and he explained to Dilly that it wasn't *his* book, it was the one that belonged in the library. It was exactly the same, but his one was safe at home. Father explained that there were thousands of copies of the same book in shops and libraries everywhere. Dilly didn't look as if he believed him.

But he did say sorry to the little dinosaur, and to the librarians, and he did help to tidy up the books that had been knocked over.

When we got home, he was sent straight up to his room as a punishment.

Later, though, at bedtime, I heard him talking to Father.

"Father," he said, "you know those other copies of *The Three Little Dinosaurs*, the ones you said were the

same as mine?"

"Yes, Dilly," said Father. "What about them?"

"Well," said Dilly, "I bet they're not as good as *my* one, are they?"

Father was quiet for a second.

"Dilly . . ." he started to say. Then I heard him sigh. "You're probably right, Dilly," he laughed. "I should think yours is the best one there is!"

11

II.   DILLY THE WORST DAY EVER

Dilly has always been naughty, but recently he's been a lot worse. It seems that Mother and Father have to tell him off and send him to his room at least two or three times a day.

Yesterday, for instance, Dilly started misbehaving as soon as he got out of bed. Mother told him to go into the bathroom to have a wash and have his teeth cleaned, but he wouldn't. He just stamped his foot and made a horrible face.

"I won't, I won't, I won't," he said. "I hate toothpaste. It's smelly and yucky!"

I thought for a moment that Mother was going to lose her temper. But she didn't. Instead, she just sighed.

"Dilly," she said, "I think you must be the naughtiest, most stubborn little dinosaur in the whole, wide world."

"I am NOT!" shouted Dilly, and stamped his foot again.

"Oh yes you are," said Mother. "Why, I don't think you could be good for a whole day if you tried."

"I could, I could!" shouted Dilly.

"All right, Dilly," said Mother. "If you think you can, why don't you prove it? Why don't you try and be good for the rest of today? And if you are good, perhaps we'll give you a little treat."

Dilly didn't shout this time. He smiled.

"What kind of treat, Mother?" he said in his softest, best behaved voice.

"Oh, I don't know, Dilly . . . " she said. "Something nice, I should think. You'll just have to wait and see. Well? Are you going to be good today?"

Dilly smiled again.

"Yes, Mother," he said. "I will." And then he marched into the bathroom, and stood by the basin, waiting to have his

teeth cleaned and to be washed.

At breakfast, Dilly ate all his fern flakes and toasted fern stalks without making any mess at all. He didn't put his elbows on the table, or knock over his pineapple juice, like he usually does. And afterwards, he helped Father to tidy everything away.

"Well, Dilly," said Father. "You are being very helpful today."

Dilly just smiled, and asked Father to pass him the next thing to put away. It was his favourite cup, the one with his name on, the one he always drank his pineapple juice from.

But as Father handed it to him, it fell

to the floor – and smashed into tiny pieces. Dilly looked upset.

"Oh, Dilly," said Father. "You must be more careful . . . still, never mind. I'll finish up here. You run along and play."

Dilly did run along and play, which was surprising. Usually he pesters Mother or Father to play with him, or let him watch cartoons on TV. But today he said he was going to play houses, and went into the garden.

Dilly isn't very patient, but he spent ages making a house. First he put a blanket down on the ground by the giant fern, and then he hung another from a branch to make a roof. He laid out all his toys, and he even said that I could play with him if I wanted to.

"My, my, Dilly," said Mother. "That looks like an interesting game. You see how much fun it can be if you spend less time being naughty and more time playing?"

Dilly smiled. He looked really pleased with himself.

But just at that moment, a big, black cloud passed over the sun. The sky went very dark, and it turned quite chilly. Then some little drops of rain began to fall. They pitter-pattered on the fern leaves and on Dilly's house. Mother said

she thought there was going to be a storm.

She was right. Soon the little drops of rain had become great fat drops that poured from the sky. We had to rush to take Dilly's house apart and get everything in before it all got soaked.

Dilly looked fed up.

"Never mind, Dilly," said Mother. "It might be sunny again later. Then you can go outside to play again."

But it didn't get sunny later. It rained, and rained, and rained. We had to stay indoors all day.

Now usually on days like that, Dilly gets bored. And when Dilly gets bored, he gets really naughty and does all the things he shouldn't. Today was different, though. He played in his room for a while, and then he came downstairs and asked Mother if there was anything he could do to help her. She looked really surprised.

"Oh . . . er . . . well, Dilly," she said, "there's nothing you can do for me at the moment. How about tidying your room?"

"I've already done that," he said with a smile.

"You have?" said Mother. "Well, as you're being so good today, perhaps you'd like to watch some TV. I think there are some cartoons on today."

"Is it *Stan the Stegosaurus?*" asked Dilly. It's one of his favourites.

"Yes, I think it is," said Mother. "I don't know why you like it so much,

Dilly . . . It's not on for a while, so you'll have to be patient."

Dilly *was* patient. He didn't pester Mother to turn on the TV, although I could see that he was getting very excited. The time for the programme came round at last. Mother switched on the TV . . . but nothing happened. There was no sound, and no picture. Mother turned it off and on again, but still nothing happened.

The TV set was broken.

Mother phoned the repair dinosaur, but he couldn't come until the next day.

So we wouldn't be able to watch TV at all.

Dilly looked so disappointed when Mother told him the bad news.

"Never mind, Dilly," said Mother. "But I tell you what . . . why don't I phone Dixie's mother and ask if Dixie can come over to play with you this afternoon?"

Dilly started smiling again. Dixie's his best friend, and he just loves to play with her.

"Oh, yes please, Mother," he said.

"OK, Dilly," said Mother. "You can be thinking of what games to play while I'm on the phone."

Mother phoned . . . but it turned out

that Dixie had a cold, and couldn't come out.

Now Dilly looked even more disappointed than ever.

"Never . . ." Mother started to say.

"I know, Mother," said Dilly. "Never mind." He went off to his room looking very fed up.

Things went from bad to worse for poor Dilly. He was still trying hard to be good, but nothing seemed to go right for him. A wheel came off one of his favourite toy dino-cars while he was playing with it. Then he tripped over a rug and bumped his snout. And finally,

when he was coming out of the kitchen, I shut his tail in the door. It looked as if it hurt quite a lot.

Normally, Dilly would have shouted and screamed and maybe even hit me. But he didn't complain at all, although I could see that he really wanted to. It was getting harder and harder for him to

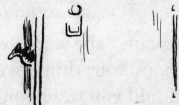

keep his temper, although Mother and Father didn't notice it – they were too busy. In fact, when Dilly tripped over the rug, Father said he hoped he wasn't going to start running around and being naughty. And when he got his tail caught in the door, Mother said he ought to look where he was going.

Later, Dilly asked if he could have a drink, and Mother gave him some pineapple juice. She put it on the table, and went out of the room. I had a drink too, and when I picked mine up, I knocked Dilly's over. There was pineapple juice all over the table, and it was dripping on to the carpet.

Then Mother came back into the room.

"Dilly Dinosaur," she said, "why do you always knock your drink over? And I thought you said you were going to be good all day today!"

"But Mother . . . " said Dilly.

"Don't you give me any of your 'buts', Dilly," she said. "Look at the mess!"

"But Mother . . . " I started to say.

"And you stay out of it, too, Dorla," she said. "Dilly, go and get a cloth immediately!"

I looked at Dilly, and he looked at me. I was going to try and tell Mother the truth, but it was too late. Before I could open my mouth, Dilly opened his . . . and fired off an ultra-special, 150-mile-per-hour super-scream. When he was quiet, Mother told him off and sent him to his room.

I managed to tell Mother the truth in the end. She went up to see Dilly while I was clearing up the spilt pineapple juice.

Dilly was very upset, she told me later. He said he had tried so hard to be good, and not to scream, but everything had gone wrong and he just couldn't keep it in any more. And now he wasn't going to get his treat.

But Mother said it wasn't his fault, and he had been very, very, very good all day. So he could have his treat after all. In fact we could *all* have a treat. Mother and Father were going to take us swamp wallowing the very next day. Dilly and I were so pleased.

And do you know what Dilly said when he went to bed?

"Mother," he said, "that was my worst day ever. Is it OK if I don't try so hard to be good tomorrow?"

"I should think so, Dilly," she laughed. "I don't know whether I could get used to you being good all the time, anyway!"

III. DILLY GOES SWAMP
WALLOWING

Mother and Father say that every young
dinosaur should learn to swamp wallow
properly. The Swamp can be a
dangerous place, and you need to learn
how to stay afloat, and what to do when
the mud's too sticky.

That's why I have swamp wallowing
lessons. I love them, too. In fact, they're
my favourite thing. I've got badges for
swamp wallowing as well – Father sewed
them on my costume.

So I was pleased when Mother said we could go to The Swamp as a treat. When we got there, the mud was lovely and warm, and Mother took me down the slide. Father wallowed with Dilly in the shallow end, and we all had a great time.

Dilly enjoyed himself so much he said he didn't want to get out when it was time to go home.

"But I'm afraid you've got to, Dilly," said Mother. "Come along, now. Don't be naughty."

Dilly didn't say anything. But I could see that he was thinking of being very naughty indeed. He opened his mouth the way he does when he's about to let loose a 150-mile-per-hour super-scream . . . then Mother said something that stopped him.

"Come on, Dilly. Let's go and ask in the office if you can start having some swamp wallowing lessons."

Dilly closed his mouth without screaming. He looked surprised.

"Lessons like Dorla has?" he said.

"Not quite like Dorla's," said Mother. "Yours will be more simple to start with. But you'll soon be wallowing just as well as her."

"No he won't," I said. "He's too silly to do it properly."

"I am not," said Dilly. "I can be just as good as you."

29

"That's enough of that, you two," said Mother. "I don't want to hear any more arguing . . . and can you hurry up now? I want to get to the office before it closes."

Dilly was still quiet when we got home.

"Aren't you excited about your lessons, Dilly?" said Father. "Once you've learned how to wallow properly you can have lots of fun. You'll be able to go down the mud slide and wallow where it's deep and warm."

Dilly didn't say anything. He didn't seem to want to talk about The Swamp, or wallowing lessons, at all. Later, when he went to bed, Mother and Father said they thought he might be nervous about having lessons.

"You were scared before your first lesson, weren't you, Dorla?" said Father. "Do you remember? It was a couple of weeks before you really started to enjoy it."

I did remember being scared. I wasn't frightened of the other little dinosaurs in my class, or the mud, or the teacher. I was scared that I would have to do something that I didn't like.

Mother and Father said they thought Dilly was scared because he didn't know what happened in a wallowing lesson. They asked me to tell him so that he would understand there was nothing to

31

be frightened of. I said I would.

But it was Dilly who asked me first. I was in my room reading *The Wind in the Giant Ferns* when I heard someone coming up the stairs, stamp, stamp, stamp, and along the landing, stamp, stamp, STAMP! Then my door flew open and went BANG! against the wall.

It was Dilly, and he had his I'm-going-to-ask-you-a-very-important-question look on his face.

"Dorla," he said.

"What, Dilly?"

"Er . . . well . . . what do you actually *do* in a swamp wallowing lesson?"

I told him that he wasn't to be frightened, because the teacher was very nice and would look after him. But I couldn't remember exactly what the very young dinosaurs did in the baby class . . . so I thought I'd tell Dilly about all the exciting things he would be able to do once he could wallow well enough to go into a class like mine.

I told him how great it was when we jumped in where the mud was really deep. I said that sometimes we went right under the mud, and came up coughing and spluttering. And last week, I said, my friend Doni didn't come up for ages. The teacher thought she'd lost her, but she came up in the end, and only cried for a little while . . .

It was funny, though. Dilly didn't look very excited by what I was telling him. In fact, he looked even more worried when he left my room . . . I couldn't understand it.

A few days later, when it was nearly time to go to The Swamp for his first lesson, Mother asked him if he would like to help pack his things.

"See, Dilly?" she said. "Here's the new outfit I bought for you. It looks really good, doesn't it? You're going to be the best-dressed little dinosaur in The Swamp in these stripes . . . "

"I won't," said Dilly. "I'll look stupid."

"Don't be like that, Dilly," said Mother. "Here's your towel, and your mud wings to help you float . . . and I've packed some Crispy Fern Flakes and a

carton of pineapple juice, too. You can
have a snack straight after you come out.
You'll probably be really hungry by
then."

"I won't," said Dilly. I thought
Mother was sure to tell him off for being
so sulky, but she didn't. When Father
took Dilly out to the dino-car, she told
me she thought he was still nervous
about his lesson.

When we got there, Mother took Dilly out of the changing room to the side of The Swamp. There he had to line up with the other little dinosaurs in his class. He looked very small, and very frightened.

The teacher said hello, and started asking them their names. As she moved down the line towards Dilly, I had a feeling I knew what was going to happen. Dilly had the look on his face he usually does when he's winding up to let loose a 150-mile-per-hour super-scream . . .

The next moment I heard a scream, a very loud scream . . . but it didn't sound like the usual scream Dilly lets rip.

Dilly was still standing there with his mouth open . . . but there was no noise coming from it. The scream was coming from the little dinosaur next to him. And

Dilly was looking at him as if he couldn't believe what he was hearing.

The little dinosaur didn't stop screaming for a long time. He wouldn't get into the mud, either, with the other little dinosaurs. He kicked and struggled, and tried to bite the teacher. He held on to the diving branch on the giant fern, and wouldn't let go.

The other little dinosaurs all behaved very well, though – even Dilly. They got into the mud and did what the teacher asked them, and the only problem was that they kept looking at the naughty little dinosaur when they should have been looking at the teacher. His father finally had to carry him away under his arm, the way Father has to carry Dilly sometimes when he's being naughty.

Once he'd gone, there was no trouble at all.

"Well, Dilly," said Mother after the lesson was over, "did you enjoy that? It looked like lots of fun."

Dilly didn't seem to be listening to Mother, though.

"Why did that little dinosaur scream so much?" he said.

"I think he was scared, Dilly," said Mother. "Weren't you when you arrived today?"

"No, Mother," said Dilly. "I wasn't scared at all."

Mother and Father said later they thought Dilly had been so interested in that other little dinosaur that he'd forgotten to be frightened himself.

"About that naughty dinosaur," I heard him say to Mother at bedtime.

"Do you think he's more naughty than me?"

"Not quite, Dilly," Mother laughed. "I don't think anyone could be as naughty as you."

Dilly didn't say anything. But Mother said he was smiling when he went to sleep . . .

IV.   DILLY AND THE CHRISTMAS PRESENTS

Christmas is my favourite time of the year. It's really terrific.

The only trouble with Christmas is . . . Dilly. He gets so excited that he almost always does something he shouldn't. And last year, he was naughtier than ever.

It started at breakfast one day. Mother said she was thinking of doing some Christmas shopping. As soon as Dilly heard Mother say 'Christmas', he looked up and said something. But none of us could understand a word.

"Dilly Dinosaur," said Father, "if I've told you once, I've told you a thousand times – you must never speak with your mouth full!"

Dilly chewed very fast, then swallowed with a gulp.

"Is it Christmas tomorrow?" he said. Mother smiled.

"No, Dilly," she said. "But it won't be long now."

"Does that mean Dino Claus will be coming soon?" Dilly said.

"Of course it doesn't, silly Dilly," I said. "Everyone knows that Dino Claus only comes on the night before Christmas."

"Now, now, Dorla," said Father. "Don't be mean to your little brother."

"Tell us, Father," said Dilly. "Tell us

about Dino Claus!" He was very excited.

Father said that Dino Claus lives in The Great Swamp with lots of helpers. They make the toys he takes to young dinosaurs all over the world. Father also explained how Dino Claus rides in a special sleigh pulled by six magic dinosaurs who can fly.

"You look a little confused, Dilly," said Mother.

"Is it a very, very, very, very big sleigh, Father?" Dilly said.

"It's quite big," said Father, "but not *that* big."

"So how does Dino Claus get all the toys in it?" asked Dilly. "You told us the other day that there are millions and billions and zillions of young dinosaurs in the world."

Father laughed.

"I don't know if there are quite that many, Dilly," he said. "But the truth is that Dino Claus only brings the little presents you find in your Christmas stocking on Christmas Day. Mothers and Fathers buy the bigger ones."

I could see that Dilly had his very thoughtful look on his face.

"Father," he said after a while, "do

you and Mother buy Christmas presents
for me . . . *before* Christmas Day?"

"Er . . . well . . . yes, Dilly," said
Father. "I just said that."

"Well," said Dilly, "what do you do
with them then?"

"We hide them away where naughty
little dinosaurs won't find them," said
Mother. "And you're not to go looking
for any presents, either. Dino Claus
only brings presents for good little
dinosaurs."

"I'll be good, Mother," said Dilly. "I
really will."

Anyway, soon it really began to feel
like Christmas. We started to get lots of
Christmas cards, and Dilly didn't do
anything bad for several days.

But as Christmas got closer and closer,
he began to act very strangely. Once or
twice I found him doing some very odd

things. I saw him looking under a rug
and peering into a vase, which he nearly
knocked over. I caught him looking
under bushes in the garden, and behind
the giant fern, and in other odd places.

But when I asked him what he was
doing, he just said . . . "Oh, nothing,"
and walked away. And whenever

Mother or Father were around, he didn't
do any looking at all.

Then one day, Mother found Dilly in
her bedroom.

"Dilly Dinosaur," I heard her say, "what are you doing? Why have you opened that drawer?"

"Er . . . I was looking for a sweater, Mother," he said. He'd gone quite green with embarrassment.

Mother looked rather cross.

"Now you know very well that *your* sweaters are in *your* drawer in *your* room, Dilly," she said. "I hope you weren't looking for any Christmas presents . . . were you?"

"Oh no, Mother," said Dilly. He went a little greener.

"Ummm . . ." said Mother. She didn't look as if she believed him. "Well just make sure you don't," she said.

"I will, Mother," said Dilly. "Er, I mean, I won't."

The next day was the day before Christmas Eve. We were going to see Grandmother and Grandfather. But when Mother was getting Dilly ready to go out, she began to sniff.

"Whatever is that smell?" she said. Father and I started to sniff too. Sniff, sniff, we all went – all of us, that is, except Dilly. And that was because the smell seemed to be coming from . . . *him*.

"Dilly Dinosaur," said Father. "What have you been up to?"

"Me, Father?" said Dilly. "I haven't done anything. I could see that he was beginning to go a little green and hot.

"Have you been touching things you're not allowed to?" said Father. "Things in the bathroom?" Dilly said nothing.

"Right," said Father. "Unless you tell me what you've done by the time I've counted to five, Dilly, you're going to be in a lot of trouble. One . . . two . . . three . . . four . . ."

Father never made it to five. Dilly opened his mouth, but all that came out was . . . an ultra-special, 150-mile-per-hour super-scream, the one that makes Father run outside and slam the door,

Mother and I dive under the table, and all the baubles on the Christmas tree explode.

When Dilly had calmed down, Mother and Father told him off. It turned out that Dilly had been looking for any

Christmas presents Father had hidden in his drawer – and he'd found one, all wrapped up. Dilly thought it was for him, but it was a bottle of perfume

Father had bought for Mother. Dilly had unwrapped it, taken the top off . . . and spilt it, mostly over himself.

Father was cross, and said that Dilly had been very, very naughty.

"You'll have to have a bath, too," he said. "You can't go out smelling like that."

But Mother said there wasn't time. We had promised to be at Grandmother and Grandfather's house by eight o'clock, and it was nearly that now.

Father gave Dilly a quick wash, but Dilly still smelt of perfume when we left. As soon as we arrived, Grandmother and Grandfather asked what the smell was. They laughed when Mother and Father told them.

But Dilly didn't laugh. He looked fed up. He also looked a little worried.

"Father," he said that night at bedtime, "will I still get some presents from Dino Claus now that I've been naughty?"

"There's still a whole day to go," said Father. "It's Christmas Eve tomorrow, and if you're good all day, Dino Claus *might* still bring you some presents . . . "

Dilly was very helpful and well-behaved on Christmas Eve. Father hung up our Christmas stockings, and said that the sooner we were asleep, the

sooner it would be Christmas Day.

He was right. When I woke up, my stocking was full of lovely Christmas presents . . . and so was Dilly's. All our presents from Mother and Father were round the Christmas tree, and we had a wonderful time opening them.

Dilly was so excited and pleased with his presents that he promised he would be good for a whole year, right up to next Christmas!

But I'm not sure whether Dilly *can* be good for a whole year.

Do you think he can?

Dilly's Muddy Day

More adventures from the naughtiest dinosaur in the world . . .

Like the day he went to the park and rode his dinotrike into the swamp. And the time he wanted more pocket money and tried to open his own shop.

Dilly Tells the Truth

You must know Dilly – he's the naughtiest dinosaur ever!

He's never out of trouble, even when he's trying to be *good*. Like the time he kept on telling the truth – although he really shouldn't have . . .

Dilly and the Horror Film

The naughtiest dinosaur in the world is staying with granny for the evening. It's movie time!

They both get a fright when the late film turns out to be a spooky one. Having a 150 mph scream can have its problems . . .

Dilly and the Ghost

After Dilly persuades Father to read him
ghost stories at bedtime, he's positive the
house is haunted. But no-one in the family
believes him. So Dilly decides to convince
everyone that there really are ghosts about
the house . . .

A Selected List of Fiction from Mammoth

While every effort is made to keep prices low, it is sometimes necessary to increase prices at short notice. Mammoth Books reserves the right to show new retail prices on covers which may differ from those previously advertised in the text or elsewhere.

The prices shown below were correct at the time of going to press.

☐	7497 0366 0	**Dilly the Dinosaur**	Tony Bradman	£1.99
☐	7497 0021 1	**Dilly and the Tiger**	Tony Bradman	£1.99
☐	7497 0137 4	**Flat Stanley**	Jeff Brown	£1.99
☐	7497 0048 3	**Friends and Brothers**	Dick King-Smith	£1.99
☐	7497 0054 8	**My Naughty Little Sister**	Dorothy Edwards	£1.99
☐	416 86550 X	**Cat Who Wanted to go Home**	Jill Tomlinson	£1.99
☐	7497 0166 8	**The Witch's Big Toe**	Ralph Wright	£1.99
☐	7497 0218 4	**Lucy Jane at the Ballet**	Susan Hampshire	£2.25
☐	416 03212 5	**I Don't Want To!**	Bel Mooney	£1.99
☐	7497 0030 0	**I Can't Find It!**	Bel Mooney	£1.99
☐	7497 0032 7	**The Bear Who Stood on His Head**	W. J. Corbett	£1.99
☐	416 10362 6	**Owl and Billy**	Martin Waddell	£1.75
☐	416 13822 5	**It's Abigail Again**	Moira Miller	£1.75
☐	7497 0031 9	**King Tubbitum and the Little Cook**	Margaret Ryan	£1.99
☐	7497 0041 6	**The Quiet Pirate**	Andrew Matthews	£1.99
☐	7497 0064 5	**Grump and the Hairy Mammoth**	Derek Sampson	£1.99

All these books are available at your bookshop or newsagent, or can be ordered direct from the publisher. Just tick the titles you want and fill in the form below.

Mandarin Paperbacks, Cash Sales Department, PO Box 11, Falmouth, Cornwall TR10 9EN.

Please send cheque or postal order, no currency, for purchase price quoted and allow the following for postage and packing:

UK   80p for the first book, 20p for each additional book ordered to a maximum charge of £2.00.

BFPO   80p for the first book., 20p for each additional book.

Overseas   £1.50 for the first book, £1.00 for the second and 30p for each additional book
including Eire   thereafter.

NAME (Block letters) ....

ADDRESS ....

....

....